THE THUD

MIKAËL ROSS

Translated by Nika Knight

Thank you to all the citizens of Neuerkerode, who welcomed me with such open arms into their community.

Thank you, especially, to Jean-Baptiste Coursaud and Claire Paq for their invaluable and patient help on this book.

—Mikael Ross

MUMSIIIE!!!

MARSH-MELLOWS ARE REEEADY!

MHM...

...DELICIOUS.

ARE THERE ANY LESS BURNT ONES?

""

THAT'S THE BEST ONE SO FAR...

SIGH...

WHAT'S 'AT?

HERE YOU GO.

FOR ME?

YES, FOR WHO ELSE? MY BIRTHDAY BOY. GO ON, UNWRAP IT!

YESSSSS!

NOW YOU DON'T HAVE TO PLAY AIR GUITAR ANYMORE.

5

MUMSIE'S SLEEPING ON THE FLOOR. BUT SLEEPING HAPPENS IN BED!

BAD.

BAD.

BAD.

AND BLOOD ... THERE'S BLOOD, TOO ... BLOOD ON THE FLOOR ... BLOOD SHOULDN'T BE THERE.

STOP. I HAVE TO CALM DOWN.

FLIP.

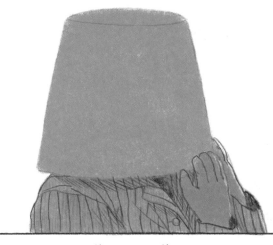

THINK... MUST THINK...

THE DOCTOR HAS TO COME ... MUMSIE CALLS THE DOCTOR ... USUALLY.

BUT NOW IS NOT USUALLY. MUMSIE CAN'T CALL HIM NOW!

NOEL HAS TO CALL THE DOCTOR.

BUT I NEED THE NUMBER ... THE RIGHT NUMBER.

BEEEEEEEEP

FISH. WAS SOMETHING ABOUT FISH...

MAYBE...

RIING RIING

CLICK

YOU'VE REACHED BERLIN EMERGENCY SERVICES. HOW CAN I HELP YOU?

THE DOCTOR!

TWO BIG GUYS COME. BEAT DOWN THE BATHROOM DOOR. WRAP UP MUMSIE INNA GOLD BLANKET. SHE LOOKS TINY IN BETWEEN THEM.

THEY DRIVE CRAZY FAST, WITH DAH-DOO DAH-DAH AND ALL THAT!

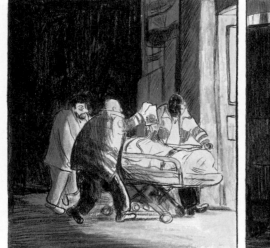

11

AND THEN? DON'T KNOW ANYMORE... MEMORY OF IT'S BROKEN.

EVERYTHING'S ALL TURNED AROUND SINCE THE THUD.
AT NIGHT, NO SLEEP. AT DAY, TIRED.

BECAUSE OF THE THUD I CAN'T LIVE AT HOME ANYMORE... THEY SAY.

HOME IS NOT MY HOME ANYMORE.

THUD, STROKE, COOOMA... I DON'T UNDERSTAND ANYMORE.

A MAN WITH A 'STACHE IS THE BOSS NOW.

WE DRIVE ON THE AUTOBAHN.

THEN A COUNTRY ROAD. WHERE'S THE 'STACHE TAKING ME?

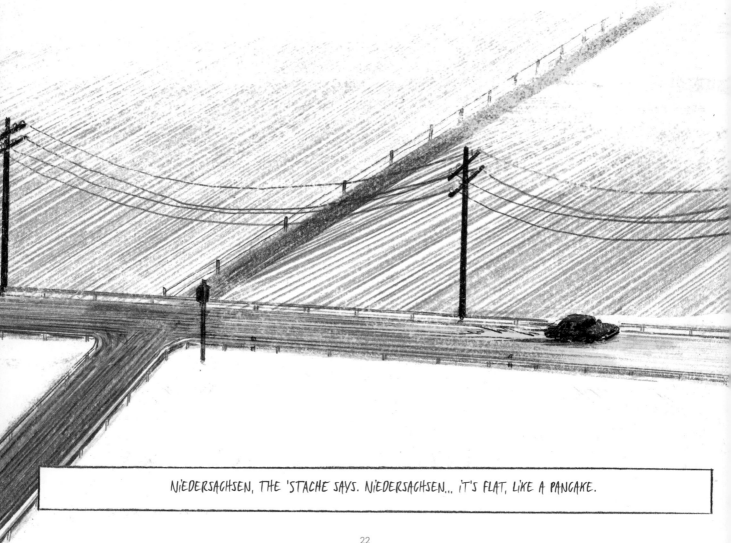

NIEDERSACHSEN, THE 'STACHE SAYS. NIEDERSACHSEN... IT'S FLAT, LIKE A PANCAKE.

DISCO

FUNNY BIRDS

THE TOODLE

THE PRINCESS

WE'RE IN OLLI'S TROOP.

OLLI IS THE POLICE INSPECTOR...

... WE'RE THE TROOP.

MEN. WE'RE SECURING THE ROAD TODAY.

YES, BUT OLLI...

NO BUTS! GENTLEMEN...

OLLI, BUT WHY IS IT WE'RE DOING THIS?

BECAUSE THE CARNIVAL IS TODAY. AND THERE EXISTS A HEIGHTENED RISK OF TERRORISM.

BOOM!

VOOM!

?

WHOOP!

VOOM!

BOOM!

EVERYONE THROWS CARAMELS THE WHOLE TIME.

LATER...

PENELOPE MARIA GARCIA.

HUH, YOU KNOW HER?

BORN IN 1988

... LIKE EMMA STONE.

AND RIHANNA.

AND ADELE.

VALENTIN WANTS TO SEARCH EVERYWHERE FOR LEFTOVER CARAMELS.

NO, IT'S NOT A NAME! EEL-ECTRIC IS A WHEN A BOY AND GIRL ARE TOGETHER...

OH, THAT'S WHAT YOU MEAN!

WHAT ARE THEY TALKING ABOUT?

I NEVER WANTED THAT. SOMETHING... WITH A BOY. WHY BOTHER?

I'D RATHER HAVE MY FREEDOM.

WHEN IS THIS BUS COMING?

IT WASN'T ALLOWED THEN, ANYWAY. TALKING TO BOYS MEANT GETTING A GOOD THRASHING.

NOTHING WAS ALLOWED THEN.

BECAUSE OF THE BIG FENCE.

HOW COME?

NOT AS SMALL AS THAT ONE THERE.

IT WENT THROUGH ALL OF NEUERKERODE. DIVIDED THE GIRLS FROM THE BOYS.

EELPORN AND THE HORNETS WANT IT THAT WAY.

WHO?

THE HORNETS. WELL, THE SISTERS. WE CALL THEM THAT. YOU HAVE TO LOOK CLOSELY. NOT ALL SISTERS ARE HORNETS. BUT MOST OF THEM ARE.

MY BROTHER LIVES ON THE OTHER SIDE OF THE FENCE.

i CAN SEE HiM SOMETIMES, DESPITE iT...

ERWiN, WHERE DiD YOU GET THAT?

GET WHAT?

THAT ARM THiNG?

i MADE iT.

WHEN WiLL MOMMY COME BACK TO ViSiT US?

HMM... DON'T KNOW...

AND WHO'S THAT?

BECAUSE GOD CANNOT DESIRE FOR SICK PEOPLE AND iNVALiDS TO REPRODUCE WiTH OTHER SiCK PEOPLE AND iNVALiDS.

ERWIN WAS RIGHT.

THEY CAME AND TOOK SO MANY OF US.

i HID. IN THE FOREST. THE HORNETS NEVER FOUND ME.

THEN CAME THE AMERICANS.
EELPORN WAS SUDDENLY GONE. JUST LIKE THAT.

AND EVEN OLD PASTOR FEHR CAME BACK.

ERWIN DIDN'T COME BACK...

THE KEVIN THING

"PONSGOTT"

FLYING AGAIN

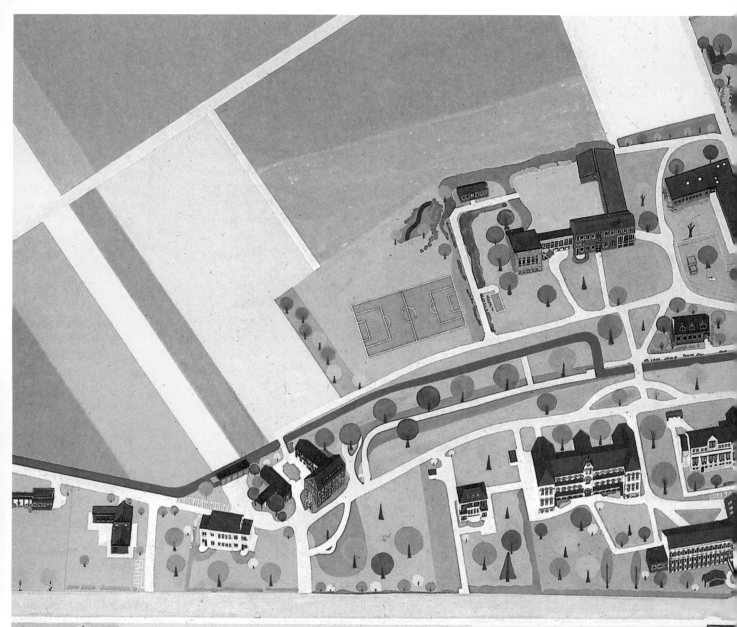

Neuerkerode

LOWER SAXONY, GERMANY • FOUNDED IN 1868

FANTAGRAPHICS BOOKS INC.
7563 Lake City Way NE
Seattle, Washington, 98115
WWW.FANTAGRAPHICS.COM

EDITOR AND ASSOCIATE PUBLISHER: Eric Reynolds
TRANSLATOR: Nika Knight
COLORIST: Claire Paq
BOOK DESIGN: Chelsea Wirtz
PRODUCTION: Paul Baresh
PUBLISHER: Gary Groth

A JUNIOR LIBRARY GUILD GOLD STANDARD SELECTION

ISBN 978-1-68396-406-3
LIBRARY OF CONGRESS CONTROL NUMBER 2020942301
FIRST PRINTING: March 2021
PRINTED IN China